The Berenstain Bears
MEET
SANTA

Special music's in the air
And Santa's at the mall
What do the little bears
Make of it all?

A FIRST TIME BOOK®

The Berenstain Bears
MEET
SANTA BEAR

Stan & Jan Berenstain

Random House 🏠 New York

Copyright © 1984 by Berenstains, Inc. All rights reserved under International and Pan-American Copyright Conventions. Published in the United States by Random House, Inc., New York, and simultaneously in Canada by Random House of Canada Limited, Toronto. *Library of Congress Cataloging in Publication Data:* Berenstain, Stan. The Berenstain Bears meet Santa Bear. SUMMARY: Sister Bear enjoys Christmas preparations, especially getting her list ready—but on Christmas morning she realizes what Christmas is really all about. [1. Christmas—Fiction. 2. Bears—Fiction.] I. Berenstain, Jan. II. Title. PZ7.B4483Bert 1984 [E] 84-4829 ISBN: 0-394-86880-3 (trade); 0-394-96880-8 (lib. bdg.) Manufactured in the United States of America 11 12 13 14 15 16 17 18 19 20

It was just two days after Thanksgiving and the sights and sounds of Christmas could be seen and heard all over Bear Country.

"It seems to me," said Mama Bear as the Bear family arrived at the Bear Country Mall, "that the Christmas season starts earlier every year."

"Yes! Isn't it great?" said Papa Bear, admiring the mall decorations.

"I'm not so sure," sighed Mama. "I'm concerned about Brother and Sister Bear. Too much excitement isn't good for cubs."

"No need to be concerned," said Papa. "Brother and Sister are good little cubs. I'm sure they'll be calm and sensible about the whole thing."

But if Papa had looked at Brother and Sister at that moment, he wouldn't have been so sure. They were passing the big new toy store, and Brother and Sister didn't look the least bit calm and sensible.

They had just come from watching Saturday morning television and there had been lots of commercials for the new Christmas toys. Sister had wanted them all...

—a bear-hug Teddy that hugged you back when you squeezed it, a ride-on pink pony, a clown-face mobile kit, and Giggly Goo, a strange substance that you could make into all sorts of funny shapes.

There had been some things that had excited Brother, too...

—especially a remote-control robot that could stand on its head, and a dinosaur molding kit.

TOY

And there they were, right in the toy store window—plus lots more! Sister was so excited, she was practically jumping up and down. And when Brother read a sign saying Santa Bear was coming to the mall to meet all his cub friends, she got even more excited.

COMING SOON
SANTA
BEAR
WILL BE HERE TO
MEET HIS FRIENDS

"Santa Bear!" she cried.
"Oh, Mama, may I come meet
Santa Bear? Please, may I?
Please?"

"In good time," said Mama,
sighing again. "Calm and
sensible, eh?" she said,
looking at Papa.

Sister Bear could hardly wait to start her Christmas list. She needed a little help from Brother with the hard words, but she didn't need any help thinking up things she wanted for Christmas!

DEAR SANTA BEAR,
This is my
CHRISTMAS List:
BEAR-HUG TEDDY
HAPPY PINK PONY
Clown ~~MoBeel~~ MOBILE
GiGGLY GOO
A RED BALL
BUBBLE PIPE
GUMBALL ~~MASHEEN~~ MACHINE
DOLLHOUSE FURNITURE
NEW D...

Over the next few days the sights and sounds of Christmas became stronger and stronger and Sister's list grew longer and longer. After a while it looked like this—

DECK THE HALLS

ELECTRIC TOY
WASHING MACHINE
COMB
AND BRUSH SET
BIRTHSTONE RING
Pink Mittens
ICE SKATES

(To see the rest of Sister's list, please turn the page.)

"You know," warned Brother, "if your list is too long, Santa Bear might think you're greedy, and not bring you anything."

Sister hadn't thought of that!

"Santa Bear has a lot of cubs besides you to think about—all the cubs in the world."

LOCKET
STORY BOOKS
COLORING BOOKS
CRAYONS

PAINTS
PAINT PAD
CLAY
Bunny PUPPET
FROGGY PUPPET

TEDDY CART
BiKE
POGO

ROLLER
SKATE
TIDDLY W
PUZZL

She hadn't thought of that, either. As she looked at her long list she began to get a little nervous.

"Have you ever met Santa Bear?" she asked Brother.

"Sure," answered Brother, who was finishing up his list—which was very short. "A couple of years ago. He asked if I'd been good, then I told him what I wanted for Christmas and gave him my list, and that was that. It was fun."

Dear Santa Bear,
For Christmas I would like a robot that can stand on its head and a dinosaur molding set and some surprises.
Thank you,
Brother Bear

Now Sister was really nervous. She thought of all the times she hadn't exactly been good...

The time she and Brother had gotten into a fight and shouted at each other.

The time Mama's best lamp had gotten broken and they told a big lie.

And the time they had let their room get so messy that Mama had threatened to throw away all their toys.

"Oh, I wouldn't worry about those times," said Mama, giving Sister a little hug. "Santa Bear doesn't expect cubs to be perfect—just good." Then she said, "I hope you have your list ready, because tomorrow is the day you are going to meet Santa Bear."

Sister gulped. "It's *almost* ready," she said. "But what about *your* list for Santa—yours and Papa's?"

"Don't worry about that, sweetie," said Papa. "Santa Bear isn't for grownups. He's just for cubs."

"Pssst!" whispered Brother. "Presents for Mama and Papa is *our* job, silly! Come on, let's see how much you've got in your piggy bank."

Sister had just enough. Brother had enough and a little extra.

That evening Sister made a new list. It looked a lot like Brother's.

When they got to Santa Bear's little house in the mall the next day, there was a line. While Sister waited she began to think about Santa and what a hard job he had. She wondered how he took care of all those cubs; she wondered where he got all those presents; she wondered…then, before she could wonder another wonder, it was her turn and she was up on Santa Bear's big lap.

SEE SANTA BEAR ENTER HERE

"It's very nice to see you," he said in a deep, jolly voice. "Now, tell me, my dear, have you been good this year?"

"Well..." said Sister, taking a deep breath, "I haven't been perfect, but I *have* been good." Then she told him what she wanted for Christmas and gave him her list.

Santa gave Sister and every other cub a souvenir coloring book. The cover showed him and his eight tiny reindeer flying through the starry night.

Sister's mind was so filled with thoughts about Santa that she almost forgot about the special shopping she had to do. But Brother remembered.

They found just the right presents for Mama and Papa. Sister chose a fine new fur-brush for Papa and a lovely new pincushion for Mama. Brother bought Mama a box of her favorite breakfast tea and, for Papa, a handy pocket calculator.

GIFT WRAP

TEA

"Look!" said Sister as they were leaving the mall. "Another Santa!" She was right. There, ringing a bell, was a rather skinny Santa with a scraggly beard. Beside him was a big iron pot that said HELP THE NEEDY.

"That's one of Santa's many helpers," explained Papa. "His job is to collect money to help the needy—birds who need seed, squirrels who didn't put enough aside for the winter."

The Bear family all put money in the pot. Sister had spent all hers and had to borrow some from Mama.

Finally the days and weeks of preparation and waiting were over and it was Christmas Eve.

"You know something, Papa?" said Sister as she helped hang the last holly wreath. "I've been thinking about Santa Bear and what a hard job he has. How can he visit every cub in the world in just a single night? Where does he get all those gifts? And besides— how can reindeer fly? And how can the sleigh land if it doesn't snow? And how can Santa come down our skinny little chimney?"

Papa took a deep breath, then looked up at the starry sky.

"I guess the answer, my dear, is that Christmas is such a special time that very special, almost magical things can happen. And the most magical thing of all is Santa Bear. I'd say he has the best job in the whole world, because the joy of giving is what Christmas is all about."

"I suppose," said Sister, "that Santa could just skip the chimney and come in the front door."

"I suppose," said Papa.

Then, before she went in, she took one last look at the starry sky. But it had clouded over. And now, instead of stars, there were snowflakes—thousands and thousands of small, silent snowflakes.

"Well," she thought. "At least that'll help with the sleigh."

When Sister woke up on Christmas morning, Bear Country was covered with a beautiful blanket of snow. And the floor beneath the Bears' Christmas tree was covered with piles of beautiful presents! What fun! What excitement! What shouting!

Then, when the excitement and shouting were over, the cubs watched Mama and Papa open *their* presents.

"What lovely, thoughtful gifts!" said Mama.

"Just what I wanted!" said Papa.

It was a very special moment. Sister knew
right then and there that Papa was right:
Santa Bear *did* have the best job in the whole
world—because the joy of giving *was* what
Christmas was all about.